K is for Kite

God's Springtime Alphabet

Written by **Kathy-jo Wargin**
Illustrated by **Kim Gatto**

ZONDER**kidz**

ZONDERVAN.com/
AUTHORTRACKER
follow your favorite authors

To my son Jake—May you always cherish the first hint of spring,
and may every day remind you of the nature of God.

—KJW

To Michael for making all things possible
and to Derek for inspiring all things.

—KG

ZONDERKIDZ

K is for Kite
Copyright © 2010 by Kathy-jo Wargin
Illustrations © 2010 by Kim Gatto

Requests for information should be addressed to:
Zonderkidz, *Grand Rapids, Michigan 49530*

Library of Congress Cataloging-in-Publication Data

Wargin, Kathy-jo.
  K is for kite / by Kathy-jo Wargin ; illustrated by Kim Gatto.
     p. cm.
  Includes bibliographical references and index.
  ISBN 978-0-310-71662-4 (hardcover : alk. paper)
  1. Spring--Religious aspects--Christianity--Juvenile literature. 2. Nature--Religious
aspects--Christianity--Juvenile literature. I. Gatto, Kim, 1970- II. Title.
  BV30.W297 2009
  242'.62--dc22
                                                        2008039282

Editor: Annette Bourland
Art direction and design: Sarah Molegraaf

Printed in China

10 11 12 13 14 15 / LPC / 10 9 8 7 6 5 4 3 2 1

As soft April showers make our hearts sing,
let's find the sweetness of God's gentle spring.

A is for April Showers

Spring brings us Bunnies and baby birds too.
Spring is the time when most everything's new.

B is for Bunnies

Small Caterpillars are nature's surprise.
When God waves his hand they become butterflies.

C is for Caterpillars

Daffodils blooming will bring us good cheer,
breaking through earth to shout "spring is here!"

D is for Daffodils

Springtime means Easter—a time to renew.
Jesus has risen—we know this is true.

E is for Easter

With family and friends we will Feast as we should.
We're thankful to God who gives all that is good.

F is for Feast

He gives us *G*rass, soft and green as it grows.
Let's take off our shoes and wiggle our toes.

G is for Grass

Or we can lie down in the meadow instead.
Look up through the clouds—Heaven's right overhead!

H is for Heaven

Springtime brings **I**nsects. It's like a parade
of God's busy creatures, each wonderfully made.

I is for Insects

Would you like a Jelly bean? They're very sweet.
It's always more fun when we share our best treat.

J is for Jelly Bean

Spring is for **K**ites, flying bright in the sky—
just like our spirits—each one soaring high!

K is for Kite

White **L**ambs in the meadow—to them all is new.
God is our shepherd, and we're his lambs too.

L is for Lamb

We can play **M**arbles. Let's gather together
to celebrate fun in God's warm springtime weather.

M is for Marble

In spring the birds flutter around without rest.
Each one is working to build its own **N**est.

N is for Nest

We'll stay Outdoors in the fresh springtime air.
A walk in the woods shows God everywhere!

O is for Outdoors

The soft little bud upon each Pussy willow
is perfectly made like a plump velvet pillow.

P is for Pussy Willow

"Quack! Quack!" says the duck to her babies in tow
as they waddle behind her in one yellow row.

Q is for Quack

The Robins are singing, and we love their song.
It's good to be joyful, so we sing along!

R is for Robin

Springtime means **S**unshine and seeds in the earth.
Each sprout shouts God's message of newness and birth.

S is for Sunshine

The tall sugar maples are ready to Tap.
Let's make maple syrup by boiling the sap.

T is for Tap

Grab your Umbrella. Here come the showers!
God's gentle rain brings forth the spring flowers.

U is for Umbrella

Like **V**iolets appearing—each one a surprise—
God's plan is blooming in front of our eyes.

V is for Violet

Do you feel the Wind blowing this way and that?
It's blowing so hard, hang on to your hat!

W is for Wind

Out of the oven a warm x-crossed bun—
an X made of icing on top of each one.

X is for X-crossed bun

Springtime brings Yard work, so it's good to ask
if our neighbors need help with an outdoor spring task.

Zing! Feel the fresh air that fills us inside.
We welcome it in with our arms open wide.

Y is for Yard Work · Z is for Zing

From sweet April showers
    that make our hearts sing,
may you feel every blessing
    of God's gentle spring!

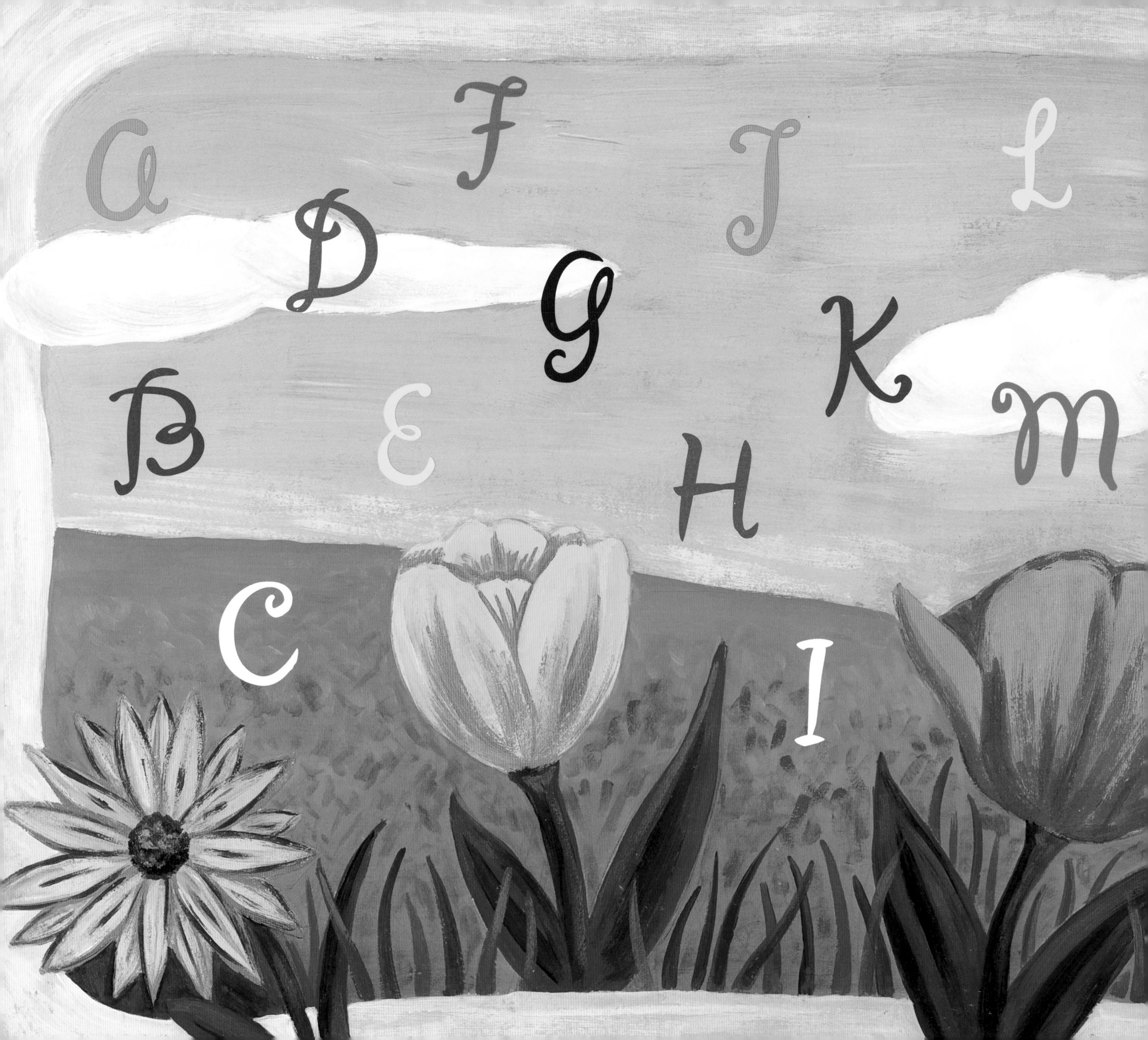
A B C D E F G H I J K L M